ROCK BOTTOM

A MIDSUMMER NIGHTMARE

ROSS MONTGOMERY

With illustrations by Mark Beech

Barrington Stoke

First published in 2020 in Great Britain by
Barrington Stoke Ltd
18 Walker Street, Edinburgh, EH3 7LP

www.barringtonstoke.co.uk

ISBN: 978-1-78112-921-0

Printed by Hussar Books, Poland

To all the exhausted,
long-suffering drama teachers:
Don't worry, it can't be as bad as <u>this.</u>

CONTENTS

1   Nick Loves Jessie   1

2   Enter Robyn   14

3   Break a Leg   22

4   The Plot Thickens   45

5   The Big Finale   51

6   All's Well That Ends Well   69

CHAPTER 1

Nick Loves Jessie

I doodled Jessie's name on my hand in biro, then I drew love hearts and flowers all around it. I'd written it on my arms too, and down both my legs. I was getting really good at it.

"Oh, Jessie!" I said with a sigh. "Love of my life, light of my soul ..."

"Nick."

I looked up. My best friend, Frank, was prodding me with his elbow and shaking his head, as usual.

"Nick?" he said. "Do you *have* to do that? People are looking at us."

Frank was right. Everyone on the bus to school was staring at me – including the driver. I could hear cars honking behind us.

"Stare all you want!" I cried, leaping up and waving my inky arms. "I LOVE Jessie, and I don't care who knows it!"

It was true. I'd been in love with Jessie Stone ever since the first day she walked into my classroom, looked me in the eyes and asked me to get out of her way. Ever since that precious moment, my feelings had grown stronger and stronger! Jessie was clever, popular and the best actor our school had ever seen. It was our destiny to fall in love, get married, say our vows on top of a mountain somewhere …

"Nick, sit down!" snapped Frank as he dragged me back to my seat. "Why do you always have to be so over the top?"

That was Frank all over. We'd been best friends since Nursery, but he'd never understood my sensitive, passionate side. He was always trying to stop me doing totally normal things, like writing Jessie epic love poems, or filling her front garden with a thousand red roses, or spelling out her name in chocolates on her desk.

"There's nothing wrong with being romantic," I said.

"You're not being romantic, you're being creepy!" said Frank. "You don't know anything about Jessie. You never even talk to her!"

I frowned. "That's not true. We talk every day!"

"She *has* to talk to you," said Frank. "You're the lunch monitor."

I sighed. "She gave me her tray yesterday. Her *tray*. I'll never forget what she said when she handed it to me: 'Put this in the bin, Rick.' Can you believe that? She knows my name! Sort of."

Frank's glasses steamed up. That always happens when he's annoyed.

"Nick – wake up. It's never going to happen. Jessie doesn't know you exist. And everyone knows she likes Blake!"

No surprises there – *everyone* liked Blake. He was the coolest boy in school, with great hair and fantastic clothes. He never said or did anything interesting, but people still thought he was amazing. He could stand up in Assembly and wet himself, and everyone would say, "Nice one, Blake" or, "Great wee, Blake" or, "Why don't you wet yourself at my house this weekend, Blake?"

"And even if Jessie *didn't* like Blake," said Frank, "she's leaving this year ... remember?"

"OF COURSE I REMEMBER!" I wailed.

Everyone turned to stare at me again.
Frank was so embarrassed, he hid behind his
bag. I couldn't help shouting. Jessie was leaving
at the end of term to go to drama school and it
hurt. The pain was still so deep and so raw. In
less than two months, the love of my life would
be gone for ever!

"Face it, Nick – it's over!" said Frank. "You
have to forget about her!"

I shook my head. How could I forget about
Jessie? I'd cried for five whole days when I heard
she was leaving, and so had our drama teacher,
Miss Plant. After all, New Forest Academy was
losing its best actor! Jessie'd had the main part
in every school play, and this term's production
of *A Midsummer Night's Dream* would be her
final performance ...

And that was how I'd come up with the best
idea of my life.

I clapped my hand on Frank's back and grinned.

"That's where you're wrong, Frank! As it so happens, I've been working on a secret plan to win Jessie's heart – a plan so brilliant, it can't fail!"

The bus pulled up to the stop, and I jumped out of my seat and ran through the school gates. Frank ran after me.

"Secret plan? What secret plan? Nick, what are you talking about?!"

I smiled. The plan had only come to me last week, but it was genius. "Remember the other day when I made you audition for a part in the school play with me ...?"

A Midsummer Night's Dream is all about people falling in love with each other. Helena loves a boy called Demetrius, but he's set to marry her best friend Hermia. Hermia doesn't want to marry Demetrius because in secret she's in love with another boy named Lysander ... it's all very complicated.

Helena				Demetrius
Demetrius				Hermia
Hermia				Lysander

They all run into a forest and fall asleep, and that's when things get *really* complicated. A naughty fairy called Puck tries to help them out and uses magic to make Demetrius fall in love with Helena ... but Puck gets the two boys mixed up! So instead of Demetrius falling in love with Helena, *Lysander* falls in love with her. That makes Hermia mad, so Puck has to fix things ... but this time Puck makes Demetrius fall in love with *Helena* too by accident! Remember – Helena already has Lysander chasing after her, crazy with love, and Hermia is so angry she and Helena end up fighting!

Lysander ♡ ♡ ♡ Helena

Demetrius ♡ ♡ ♡ Helena

Hermia ⚔ ⚔ ⚔ Helena

See, I told you it was complicated!

Luckily it all gets sorted in the end. At last everyone is happy and matched up, and they all celebrate by going to a big wedding.

There are lots of other characters, too – like an idiot named Bottom, whom Puck turns into a donkey for a joke. He's not important, just a terrible actor who puts on a play for the wedding with his friends, and it's so bad that everyone laughs at them!

I didn't care about any of those stupid joke characters – what I cared about were the main romantic boy parts. Jessie was bound to get cast as one of the girls, Hermia or Helena. If I could get cast as Demetrius or Lysander, I'd get *weeks* of rehearsing love scenes with her! I would amaze her with my acting skills, and Jessie would finally understand that we're a perfect match, and fall head over heels in love with me, and forget all about leaving school, and we could get married on a mountain somewhere. Simple!

By the time I finished telling him about the plan, Frank's glasses were so steamed up they looked like they'd been covered in Tippex.

"Nick," he moaned, "that is the *stupidest* plan I've ever heard! Jessie's not going to fall in love with you just because you're a good actor!!"

I shook my head. "Wrong again, Frank! This is my chance to show her my sensitive, romantic side. I'm sick of her treating me like a big joke while guys like Blake get all the attention – it's time for my turn in the spotlight!" I grabbed his arm. "Quick! Miss Plant will have put up the cast list. Let's see which part she gave me!"

Frank groaned. "Fine – but if it doesn't work, promise me you won't get upset and start wailing again ..."

Frank didn't need to worry – I had aced my audition, saying my lines as loudly as I could, waving my hands a lot and crying real tears, with snot and everything. Miss Plant said she had the *perfect* part for me. That must mean I was Demetrius or Lysander!

Sure enough, the cast list was up outside the drama studio. I pushed aside the crowds, desperate to see which parts everyone had:

```
Ruby .............. HERMIA

Jessie ............ HELENA
```

I gasped – Jessie was Helena! That was perfect – she had romantic scenes with Demetrius *and* Lysander! I looked down to see which boy I had been cast as:

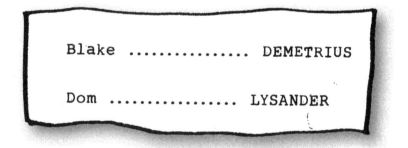

```
Blake .............. DEMETRIUS

Dom .............. LYSANDER
```

I blinked. "Wait – what's going on? Where's my name?"

"It's, er ... down there," said Frank quietly.

He pointed down the list – *right* down. My heart froze. There was my name all right, but it wasn't next to the part I was expecting.

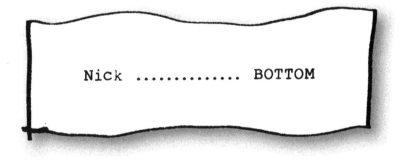

```
Nick  .............  BOTTOM
```

CHAPTER 2

Enter Robyn

"Nick, please stop."

I'd been wailing under the school's weeping willow ever since I heard the bad news. I always came here to wail when I was upset.

"It's no use, Frank!" I cried as I punched my fists against the tree trunk. "The plan's ruined!"

It was all too much to take. I'd wanted to show Jessie that I was a sensitive, romantic hero. Instead, I'd been given the part of Bottom, a bumbling idiot who spends half the play turned into a donkey.

"Jessie will never fall in love with me in ... *these*!" I sobbed.

I pointed at the huge furry donkey ears that stuck out of the top of my head. Miss Plant had made everyone try on their costumes.

"They're not so bad," Frank muttered. "At least *you* don't have to wear a dress."

He pointed at the beautiful ballgown he was wearing. Frank had been given the part of Flute, one of Bottom's terrible actor friends, who acts as a girl in their dreadful play. Frank and I were even going to share an onstage kiss! Not only had my plan to win Jessie's heart failed, now Frank and I were going to look like idiots in front of the whole school as well.

"I just don't understand it," I moaned. "I gave the audition of my life! Why did Miss Plant make me Bottom ...?"

"Ahem."

I looked up. Someone was sitting in the branches of the willow, ripping up school books and throwing away the pages.

"Go away, Robyn," I groaned. "I'm not in the mood!"

Robyn was the naughtiest girl in school. She was always getting into trouble for something: filling the swimming pool with jelly, throwing watermelons at the ceiling fan during Assembly, releasing a herd of pigs into the staff room ... Miss Plant had given her a backstage job in the play so she could keep a close eye on her at all times.

"Let me make sure I heard you right," said Robyn as she jumped out of the tree. "You have *no idea* why Miss Plant cast you as Bottom."

I shook my head. "I asked to be Demetrius or Lysander ..."

"Ahhhh!" said Robyn. "The main boy parts, which went to Blake and Dom – the two coolest kids in school. Who can't even tie their shoelaces, let alone act."

I blinked. "What's your point?"

Robyn rolled her eyes. "Can't you see, Nick? This play has got nothing to do with talent! Miss Plant just gave all the best parts to the cool kids so she can look good in front of the parents!"

I gasped. She was right! Jessie's best friend Ruby was Hermia, and her other friend Claire was Puck. These were both big parts, but neither of them could act their way out of a paper bag. Meanwhile, all the stupid parts – like the "bad actors" who put on the play with Bottom – had been given to the class outcasts. Quince had been given to Petra, who only ever talked about frogs. Starveling had gone to Taylor, who cut her own hair. Snout was played by Tomi, who always smelled of egg sandwiches. And the part of Snug had been given to Leo, who ate his own bogies.

"But that's not fair!" I cried. "This was my chance to win Jessie's heart! Now she'll *never* see what an amazing romantic actor I am ..."

Robyn smiled.

"Oh, there's still a chance! As it so happens, I have a foolproof plan that will help you take Blake's part on the night of the play *and* win Jessie's heart before the end of term, and it won't cost you a penny ..."

My heart lifted ... but then I felt the cold, steady hand of Frank on my shoulder.

"Don't be stupid, Nick. This is Robyn you're dealing with! The naughtiest kid in school! She's just going to get you in trouble!"

Robyn looked offended. "I'm only trying to help a friend! And, you know, ruin Miss Plant's play." She shrugged. "What can I say? I'm only human."

Frank gave me one of his looks.

"It's not worth it, Nick. You don't need to take Blake's part to get what you want. Why don't you just *talk* to Jessie and tell her how you feel?"

I thought about it. Frank was always Mr Sensible – but love isn't sensible. Sometimes, if you want to follow your heart, things need to get a little messy.

"It's no use, Frank. If I go on stage as Bottom, Jessie will just think I'm a joke!"

I squeezed his hand. "You'll help me, won't you? As my best, best friend in all the world?"

Frank groaned and looked down at his feet. "Fine! I'll help. But only so I can stop you from doing something stupid!"

I gave him a massive hug. "Frank, you're the best!"

"Great!" said Robyn. "Now, let me explain all about my plan ..."

CHAPTER 3

Break a Leg

FOUR WEEKS LATER

It was the night of the play. The school stage was covered in big fake wooden trees and four big golden thrones for the main characters. Everyone was packed into the backstage area, getting into their costumes and putting on make-up. Nerves were at fever pitch. We only had twenty minutes left until the play started.

Just enough time to put Robyn's plan into action.

"Ready, everyone?" I whispered.

My crew ran up. It had been Robyn's idea to ask Petra, Taylor, Tomi and Leo to help us. They were just as annoyed as we were about getting bad parts, and we'd had weeks in rehearsals together to practise the plan.

I turned to Petra and Taylor. "Have you got the itching powder?"

"The itchiest on the market!" said Petra as she held up a giant bottle of SCRATCH ME IF YOU CAN.

"They use it on bears," said Taylor.

I gave them a thumbs up. "Remember the plan – you're going to put some in Ruby's costume so that she makes a big fuss. She's so loud, everyone will be looking at her! That way, Leo can get Blake out of the room and no one will notice." I turned to Leo. "Remember what

you're going to say to Blake so that he looks in the cupboard?"

"BLAKE, LOOK AT THIS COOL CUPBOARD," said Leo, hungrily probing his nose for bogies.

I nodded. We had spent weeks getting those lines perfect – Leo wasn't exactly the smartest kid in class. "Perfect! Tomi will slam the door shut when Blake looks inside …"

"And then I pull off the door handle so he can't get out again!" said Tomi, and sprayed me with a mouthful of eggy sandwich.

I wiped my face. "Brilliant! When no one can find him, I'll offer to step in and take his place at the last second. Then I'll wow the crowds with my amazing performance and make Jessie fall head over heels in love with me!"

The plan was foolproof. Frank and I were going to stay in plain sight so no one suspected we had anything to do with the way things were going, and Robyn was on lookout to make sure Miss Plant didn't see anything. By the time anyone worked out where Blake was, I'd already be on stage and winning Jessie's heart! I had spent *weeks* learning Blake's part as well as my own, until I knew it better than the back of my hand. Even better, Miss Plant would have no choice but to cut Bottom's play. That meant Frank wouldn't have to make an idiot of himself either!

"Nick, are you sure you want to do this?" said Frank, giving me a worried look. "If it goes wrong, you could get in serious trouble."

I gulped. I had to admit that I was feeling pretty nervous.

"It can't fail!" I insisted. "We've been practising for weeks now – so long as everything goes the way we planned ..."

"Everyone, quick! Over here, please!"

Miss Plant, the drama teacher, ran back in. She was looking much smarter than normal – her explosion of hair had been brushed, sort of, and she'd even ironed her shirt – and she was trembling with excitement. The entire cast crowded around her.

I turned to my gang. "Quick! Everyone's distracted – go and put the itching powder in Ruby's costume while no one's looking!"

Petra and Taylor ran off, and Tomi and Leo got into position by the cupboard. Frank and I pushed to the front of the crowd to hear what Miss Plant was saying.

"I've just been given some important news!" she said. "We're going to have a very special visitor in the audience tonight – *the Mayor himself* will be watching your performance!"

Everyone gasped. The Mayor had never come to see a play at New Forest Academy before – this really was special!

"That means tonight's performance has to go *perfectly*!" said Miss Plant. "This is a huge opportunity for me ... I mean, for you! So remember your lines! Pronounce your vowels! Project your voice to the back of the room!"

"I wish someone would project *her* to the back of the room," muttered Robyn.

Miss Plant clapped her hands. "Break a leg, everyone! We've only got fifteen minutes left. Where are my leading couples – Jessie? Ruby? Dom? Blake?"

Jessie and Ruby walked up beside her, but that was it. Miss Plant looked around.

"Dom? Blake? Where's Blake? Has anyone seen Blake?!"

I grinned – it looked like Leo and Tomi had already locked Blake in the cupboard, and we hadn't even had to use the itching powder to distract anyone! The plan had gone even better than expected. I coughed.

"Oh, how strange!" I said loudly. "I think I saw Blake running out the back door saying that he was moving to China or something ..."

"Here, Miss."

Blake walked up, staring down at his phone. Miss Plant groaned.

"Blake! How many times have I told you? Put that phone down and pay attention!"

My mouth fell open – Blake was still here! Right then, Leo and Tomi came racing back.

"We did it! Blake's in the cupboard!" said Leo.

"And we broke off the handle, just like you asked!" said Tomi proudly.

My eyes boggled. "What are you talking about? Blake's right there!"

Leo frowned. "*That's* Blake? I thought that was Dom."

I gawped. "No! How do you not know who Blake is?! You've been in the same class as him all year!" My face fell. "Wait! If Blake's here, who have you trapped in the cupboard ...?"

Miss Plant was spinning around. "Where's Dom? Has anyone seen Dom?! DOM!"

My stomach did a backflip. Leo and Tomi had trapped Dom in the cupboard instead of Blake!

"What do we do?!" I cried. "We can't tell anyone where he is – we'll be found out!"

"Can you take Dom's part?" said Frank. "Do you know his lines?"

I shook my head. "I only learned Blake's!"

Meanwhile, Miss Plant looked like she was having a heart attack. Jessie grabbed her sleeve.

"We can't do the play without Dom," she said. "We'll have to cancel the performance!"

Miss Plant started sweating. She clearly didn't want to lose her chance to impress the Mayor. "N-no – the show must go on! I'll cut Dom's part, and we'll work around him!"

Jessie frowned. "But he's one of the main characters. How can we work around him? The play won't make any sense!"

Miss Plant shushed her. "We'll make it up! I've written *hundreds* of plays in my time – nothing a few clever re-writes won't fix!" She turned to Robyn. "Robyn – take Dom's throne off stage. We don't need it any more – you can put it in the front row for the Mayor. He'll have the best seat in the house!"

With that she started going over her script with a red pen and raced into her office. I grabbed Robyn.

"What do we do? The whole plan's turned to poo! Blake's still going on stage!"

Robyn shrugged. "A mere hiccup. There's still plenty of time to take Blake out of the picture! We'll just have to find another way to get rid of him ..."

Robyn looked around. She spotted it first – a wooden trapdoor in the middle of the stage.

"There! That trapdoor opens into the basement – if Blake falls down it, he'll be stuck under the stage until the play's over. You can take his place and no one will be able to do anything about it!"

Frank was shocked. "What if he gets hurt?"

Robyn snorted. "It's just a small drop onto a stack of gym mats. He'll have a soft landing and be a little dazed, that's all! I'll go and open the trapdoor, and you find a way to make him walk across the stage. He'll be so busy looking at that stupid phone of his, he won't even notice the trapdoor's there!"

Robyn ran on stage and grabbed the throne like Miss Plant asked, then sneaked off to open the trapdoor. I ran off to get Blake ... but Frank grabbed my arm.

"Nick, no! This is going way too far! You could hurt him!"

I shook my head. "I have to do this, Frank! If I miss this chance, I'll lose the love of my life and we'll both make complete idiots of ourselves. It's just a little fall! What's the worst that could ha—"

"AAAAAAAAARGH!"

Everyone swung round. Ruby was running out of the drama studio, scratching at her dress like she was covered in a million fleas.

"MY COSTUME!" she screamed. "WHY IS IT SO ITCHY?!?"

I jumped – she really *was* loud. Petra and Taylor were suddenly back, looking pleased with themselves.

"Sorry we took so long!" said Petra. "We didn't know how much powder to sprinkle in her costume because the instructions were in Turkish ..."

"So we just used the whole bottle," said Taylor.

I almost choked. "THE WHOLE BOTTLE ...?!"

No wonder Ruby looked like she was on fire – she was covered in enough itching powder to fell an elephant! I watched as she charged across the stage, itching herself into a frenzy ...

Just as the trapdoor opened in front of her.

"NO!" I cried.

But it was too late. Ruby fell through the trapdoor like a sack of spuds. Everyone gasped and ran to the trapdoor. Ruby lay on the mats below, clutching her ankle. Miss Plant suddenly appeared beside us with her hands full of bits of torn script.

"Ruby! What are you doing down there?!" she cried.

"My ankle!" Ruby groaned. "I think I've twisted it!"

Miss Plant let out a terrible wail. "Now we've lost Hermia too! Why is this happening to me?!" She pulled herself together. "It … it's fine! The show must go on! I'll cut Ruby's scenes and re-write them!"

Jessie looked horrified. "Are you serious? We've lost two of the four main parts! You can't fix that!"

But Miss Plant wasn't listening. "Robyn! Take away Ruby's throne too! Does anyone have a spare red pen?"

She ran off, ripping out pages of script and howling. Jessie stormed off after her just as Robyn came back in, rubbing her hands.

"So! How did it go?"

I grabbed her. "It's even worse than before! Now Ruby's hurt, Blake's *still* going on stage, and we've only got ten minutes left until the play starts!"

Robyn waved me quiet. "Calm down! There's still lots of time to take Blake's place.

I happen to have a genius idea to make him leave the play all by himself, without anyone getting hurt ..."

Frank and I looked blank.

"Isn't it obvious?" said Robyn. "*Stage fright!* Make Blake too freaked out to go on stage, then you can step in and take his place!"

I gasped. She was right – by now, Miss Plant was so desperate for the play to go ahead, she'd agree to anything! I turned to Robyn, Frank, Petra, Taylor, Tomi and Leo.

"Right – I'm doing this myself. No more mistakes this time! I'm not having *anyone else* mess this up for me!"

I ran over to Blake, who was still staring at his phone. The rest of the cast were waiting beside him, ready for the play to begin and peeking nervously through the curtains.

"Hi, Blake!" I said. "Nice phone!"

He looked up. "Oh. Hi, Neville."

I smiled. "It's Nick, actually. So ... excited about the play? It must have been really hard, learning all those lines. Wouldn't it be sooooo embarrassing to forget them when you're on stage?"

Blake looked confused. "Er ... sure."

"It happens all the time!" I said. "You walk on stage, those bright lights hit you, you see all those hundreds of faces, and BAM! Your mind goes blank! That would be *terrible*, wouldn't it, Blake?"

Blake didn't look frightened – he didn't even look bothered. The other kids seemed far more worried than he did.

"You ... you don't think that's going to happen tonight, do you?" said Claire, the girl who was playing Puck.

"Oh, definitely!" I said. "After all, there are HUNDREDS of parents watching – as well as all the kids and teachers. And don't forget the Mayor! THE MAYOR!! Think of that, Blake – forgetting your lines in front of the Mayor! How bad would that be?"

Blake just shrugged. Why did he have to be so cool?! I gritted my teeth – I *had* to frighten him!

"Let's face it, we all know this play's going to be a disaster!" I said. "We've already lost two lead characters and no one knows what's happening. We're all going to be the laughing stock of the whole school! Everyone's going to point at us and say how stupid we are ..."

I was cut off by the sound of crying around me – *lots* of crying. I gasped. The rest of the

cast were sweating and shaking with fear.
Some were even racing to the toilet.

"Mummy! Help!"

"I ... I don't feel so good ..."

"I don't want to go on stage!"

My face fell. I'd managed to give the entire cast stage fright, *except* Blake! Miss Plant ran up, with Jessie close behind. They looked at the crowds of sobbing, fainting, puking children, and their faces turned white.

"It's a stage-fright epidemic!" cried Jessie. "This is the final straw – we have to cancel the play!"

Miss Plant's left eyelid twitched. By now her hair was falling out in tufts and her face was covered in streaks of red pen. She was a woman on the edge.

"No – the show must go on! I promised the Mayor a play, and I'm giving him one even if it kills me!"

Jessie finally lost her temper. She grabbed Miss Plant and shook her.

"The show *can't* go on! We've lost the entire cast!"

Miss Plant looked around with desperation –
and saw me and the rest of my crew. She
pointed at us and gave an enormous smile.

"No, we haven't!" she said. "Look! We still
have Bottom and the rest of the rubbish actors.
We'll just do their scene. Bottom will be the
star of the show!"

I gasped. "What? No ...!"

But it was too late. Miss Plant went back to work on her script, ripping out entire scenes and scribbling in new lines with red pen. Jessie shot me a filthy look.

"Thanks a lot, Rick," she said. "I saw you talking to Robyn earlier. This has been your plan all along, hasn't it? You've wrecked my last play at the school so you can take all the limelight for yourself!"

I shook my head. "N-no, that's not true! I never ..."

But Jessie wasn't listening to me. She took Blake's hand. "Come on, Blake. Let's go."

Blake looked up from his phone. "Huh? Oh yeah, cool. Bye, Neil."

I watched the love of my life walk off, hand in hand with Blake. My heart sank.

"It ... it's Nick," I whispered.

CHAPTER 4

The Plot Thickens

I sat on stage on one of the two remaining thrones, under the big wooden tree, gazing at the donkey ears in my hand. Through the crack in the stage curtains I could make out hundreds of parents waiting for the play to begin. I could even see the Mayor in the front row, wearing his chains of office and shuffling on his stage throne. In five minutes, I was going to make a complete idiot of myself in front of all of them.

But that was *nothing* compared to the pain of my broken heart.

"Nick? Are you OK?"

Frank came over and sat on the throne beside me. I shook my head.

"No, Frank," I said. "I'm even worse off than I was before. Jessie *still* doesn't know who I am, but now she hates me."

Frank patted me on the back. "I'm sorry, Nick. But maybe it's for the best. To be honest, I don't think the plan was ever going to work ..."

"You're not giving up *now*, are you?"

We turned around. Robyn was standing in the shadows at the back of the stage, rubbing her hands and grinning.

"We've still got five minutes left," she said. "That's plenty of time to turn things around!"

Frank jumped up. "Oh no you don't! You've done enough damage for one day!"

"He's right, Robyn," I said glumly. "Even if I *did* take Blake's place now, it makes no difference. I'll never win Jessie's heart."

"I disagree!" said Robyn. "You might not be able to take Blake's place any more ... but you *can* get your revenge on him."

I blinked. "Revenge? Why?"

Robyn stepped out of the shadows, her eyes glinting.

"Why should *you* be the only one to look stupid, Nick? This is your chance to get even and make *Blake* look like an idiot for a change!"

Frank gasped. "That's it! You've gone too far this time, Robyn!"

But something inside me boiled up. Robyn was right – guys like Blake always got what they wanted, while I was treated like a joke. Just for once, I wanted to be on top.

"She's right, Frank," I said. "It's time *I* got to laugh at someone. From now on, it's no more Mr Nice Nick!"

Frank's glasses steamed up. A tear ran down his cheek.

"You know what, Nick? Maybe you're *not* so nice. Blake's never done anything to you – nor has Ruby or Dom. All you care about is yourself. Maybe *that's* why Jessie doesn't like you." He picked up his skirts. "Well, I'm having no part in this. From now on, you're on your own. See you on stage!"

And with that, Frank stormed off. I was about to call after him, but something inside made me stop myself. Frank was always trying to hold me back. Well, I wasn't going to let him do that any more.

"Are you ready, Nick?"

I turned to face Robyn. I had just lost the love of my life *and* my best friend. Of *course* I was ready. I had nothing left to lose.

Robyn's eyes lit up. "Remember the big finale?"

I certainly did. Miss Plant had blown almost the entire school budget on it. At the end of the play, a confetti cannon was going to shoot brightly coloured confetti over the audience. It was so powerful that even on its lowest setting, the confetti could hit the back of the hall.

"The cannon's hidden at the back of the stage," said Robyn. "What if we *moved* it?

Say to ... under the throne where Blake will be sitting? And what if we turned the nozzle around, so it fires up at Blake instead of out at the audience ...?"

I gasped. Blake would be sitting right in the middle of the stage – the entire audience would be watching as the cannon exploded, covered him in confetti and made him scream. He'd be the laughing stock of the whole school!

I smiled an evil grin.

"Let's do it," I said. "Time to turn this *Midsummer Night's Dream* into a nightmare!"

CHAPTER 5

The Big Finale

The lights went down – the audience muttered with excitement. I stood in the wings, waiting to go on stage. Robyn leaned in close to me and whispered.

"It's all done – I got Leo to put the cannon under Blake's throne. He's going to go up like a rocket!"

I grinned. The bottom of the thrones were covered by cardboard painted with gold paint.

No one would see the cannon hidden beneath one of them.

I frowned.

"Wait – *Leo?* What if he's made another mistake and put it under Jessie's throne by accident?!"

Robyn shook her head. "No chance! I told him to put it under the one in front." She pointed to the first of the two thrones. "That's Blake's one! And even if Blake *does* sit on the wrong one, I can stop the cannon before it goes off."

It was too late to turn back now – the stage lights came on. Miss Plant waved her arms at Blake and Jessie.

"*Go!*" she snapped.

Jessie stormed on stage, with Blake close behind. I wasn't surprised she was angry – after

Miss Plant had made her final cuts to the script, Jessie didn't have many lines left.

JESSIE: *Oh, what a lovely Midsummer Night's Eve this is.*

BLAKE: *Yes.*

JESSIE: *Let's go and watch that really bad play.*

BLAKE: *Yes.*

[Jessie and Blake sit on their thrones.]

The audience muttered to each other. What was going on? The play didn't really make any sense now that Miss Plant had made her changes. All that was left was the scene with Bottom's terrible play, *Pyramus and Thisbe.*

I sighed. It was time for me to make a complete idiot of myself.

Bottom's play is supposed to be the worst play in the world. The acting is terrible, the writing is dismal, and the love story is ridiculous. Bottom's given himself the main part of Pyramus, the young soldier who's not allowed to see his lover, Thisbe. Each night, Pyramus and Thisbe meet in secret at the bottom of their garden and speak through a hole in the wall. The two lovers agree to run away and get married, but at the last second Thisbe gets chased away by a lion and Pyramus thinks she's been eaten, so he kills himself. When Thisbe comes back and finds his body, she kills herself too.

See? I *told* you it was bad.

I looked over at Frank, who was standing on the other side of the stage. He was going to be playing Thisbe, my onstage girlfriend, but he looked away when he saw me. My heart stung. Playing this scene was embarrassing enough to begin with, but now Frank was angry at me it was going to be torture.

I walked slowly on stage, and almost at once the audience started to giggle. I didn't have to wear the donkey ears any more, but Miss Plant had made sure my Pyramus costume was as stupid as possible too, with a big fake beard and bushy eyebrows. Even Blake was sniggering. I gritted my teeth. Blake was sitting on the correct throne. That made me feel better. In just a few short minutes, a thousand pounds of confetti was going to go off right beneath his bum.

You won't be laughing soon, Blake, I thought.

I threw my hands into the air and gave my best dramatic wail. Time to get this over with.

NICK: *O grim-looked night,*
         O night with hue so black!

         O night which ever art when day
         is not!

O night, O night! Alack alack alack,

I fear my Thisbe's promise is forgot!

And thou, O Wall, O sweet and lovely Wall ...

Tomi walked on stage. She was playing the part of the Wall, and her costume was even more stupid than mine: she just had a brick tied to her head. The audience hooted with laughter. I turned bright red and kept going – the quicker I got through this scene, the quicker I could get my revenge.

NICK: *And thou, O Wall, O sweet and lovely*
           Wall,

           That stand'st between her father's
           ground and mine.

           Thou Wall, oh Wall, oh sweet and
           lovely Wall,

           Show me thy chink to blink through
           with mine eye!

Tomi held up a big plastic hula-hoop – a "chink" for me to look through. The audience laughed again – even the Mayor was chuckling at how bad the play was. I couldn't take much more of this. I decided to jump ahead, so the scene would be over with as soon as possible.

NICK: *Thisbe!*

Frank wasn't expecting that – he raced on stage, screeching his lines in a high squeaky voice.

FRANK: *My love! Thou art my love, I think ...*

Frank tripped on his own skirts and went sprawling across the stage, knocking over Tomi by accident. The audience fell about laughing – I felt ready to die inside. Frank and Tomi picked themselves up, and we got through the rest of our scene together, but it was tricky when Frank couldn't even bring himself to look at me.

Then came the awkward bit. Our onstage kiss.

NICK: *Oh, kiss me through the hole of this vile wall!*

Frank and I looked at each other and grimaced.
Then we both leaned in to give each other a big
fake smooch through the hula-hoop. I had never
felt so embarrassed in my life.

Then something very strange happened.

The audience *cheered*.

I looked up in surprise. All the parents and teachers were clapping and laughing, but they weren't laughing *at* us – they thought we were funny! Frank and I couldn't believe it. We finished our scene and left the stage, the audience clapping and cheering us all the way. We stared at each other.

"They like us!" said Frank.

"They *love* us!" I said.

And they didn't just like *us*, either. Onstage, Taylor was being the Moon, waving around an old torch, and then Leo was the lion that kills Thisbe. He was dressed in a shabby fur coat. Their lines were so wooden and bad, the people in the audience were beside themselves with laughter. When Frank ran on stage to be attacked and chased by the lion, I could even see the Mayor slapping his legs and wiping away tears.

Frank did look funny in his big ballgown and terrible make-up. I'd been so busy with our plan over the last four weeks that I hadn't noticed how funny we were. We were a real hit!

It was time for my big death scene. This time I marched on stage full of confidence. The audience were already grinning from ear to ear. I saw Thisbe's torn "mantle" on the ground and gasped. I gave my loudest, hammiest acting.

NICK: *Eyes, do you see?*

          How can it be?

          O dainty duck! O dear!

          Thy mantle good,

          What, stained with blood?

I pulled out my wooden sword and jabbed it in between my arm and my body as I cried my final lines.

NICK: *Now die, die, die, die, die!*

I fell to the ground with a gurgle – and the audience cheered again. I couldn't believe it. They didn't think I was an idiot … they loved me. The Mayor was still laughing along, and Miss Plant looked absolutely delighted …

The only person who wasn't happy was Jessie. And who could blame her? She was right – I had ruined her night. I had done all this to win her heart, but I hadn't once thought about *her* feelings. And as for Blake …

My heart froze.

The cannon!

I had forgotten all about it. At the end of this scene, it was going to blast him right off his throne. I looked around to catch Robyn's eye, but she had vanished. Frank was already on stage to say his final lines. I had made a terrible mistake – I had to stop it!

Frank lifted his fake dagger and raised it up to stab himself …

FRANK: *And, farewell, friends.*

Thus Thisbe ends.

Adieu, adieu, adieu.

"NOOOOOOO!" I shouted.

I leapt up. The audience chuckled along, thinking this was all part of the joke. Frank stared at me, trying to work out what was going on.

"Nick? What are you doing?" he hissed.

There was no time to explain. I threw myself across the stage and shoved Blake off his throne, then leapt on top of it to protect Jessie from the explosion. I covered my face and clamped my eyes shut, waiting for the colossal bang to cover me in confetti ...

It didn't come. I opened my eyes. The audience were looking confused. Miss Plant was furious. Beside her were Robyn and Leo, staring at me blankly. I tore off the cardboard bottom of the throne ... but there was nothing there.

"Er ... what's going on?" I said to Robyn. "Where's the confetti cannon?"

"Don't look at me!" said Robyn. "I told Leo to put it under the throne at the front ..."

"I *did!*" said Leo. "That one over there!"

Leo pointed. But he wasn't pointing at the throne beneath me – he was pointing to the one in the front row.

The one the Mayor was sitting on.

"See?" said Leo. "The one at the front! Just like you s—"

KABOOM!

The explosion filled the theatre like a thunderclap.

I gasped – the cannon under the Mayor's throne had gone off. A huge cloud of smoke and confetti filled the hall. But the cannon was far, far more powerful than we had thought.

The blast had lifted the Mayor's throne clear off the ground – and not just by a few inches. We all stared as the Mayor shot over our heads and across the stage with a trail of rainbow confetti behind him ...

THUNK!

The force of the explosion jammed him into the branches of the wooden tree, his legs kicking and his voice roaring with anger. The cannon blast had even blown a smoking hole in his trousers, so we could all see his big spotted underpants. The smoke had set off the fire alarms, so water was spraying down from the overhead sprinklers. The audience were coughing and spluttering and racing for the exits.

"Er ... Robyn?" I asked. "What power setting did you change the cannon to?"

"The highest one," she said. "And I also might have, er, fiddled with the insides a bit too ..."

"NOOOO! YOUR MAJESTY!"

Miss Plant raced onto the stage and started trying to grab the Mayor's legs as they kicked in the fake wooden tree.

"PLEASE FORGIVE ME, YOUR HIGHNESS …"

She got hold of one of his legs and heaved with all her might. There was a comical TWANG. Then another, and another – all the wires which held the tree in place were snapping. With an enormous groan, the tree collapsed onto the stage, ripping down the curtains and stage lights and landing on top of Miss Plant like a ton of bricks.

We stood on the stage in shocked silence. There was nothing any of us could say.

"I think we, er … might be in trouble," I said.

Blake held up his phone and took a picture.

CHAPTER 6

All's Well That Ends Well

We stood on the playing fields, soaking wet and covered in confetti. The rest of the audience watched as the fire brigade turned off the sprinklers and carried the Mayor and Miss Plant out of the hall on stretchers.

"Well!" said Robyn. "I thought that went OK."

We all stared at her. She held up her hands.

"What?! You lot were the stars of the show, and I got to ruin Miss Plant's play. I call that a success!"

"You idiot," said Frank. "You blew up the Mayor and flattened Miss Plant! All seven of us are going to be expelled when they work out what we've done ..."

"No, you won't," I said.

The others turned to me. What was I on about? I stepped forward.

"Where are you going?" Frank groaned. "You're not going to swoon under the weeping willow again, are you?"

I shook my head. "No, Frank. No one's swooning tonight. There's something much more important I need to do."

I walked over to where Miss Plant was being lifted into an ambulance, bruised and muttering. I gulped – this wasn't going to be easy, but I had to do it.

"Miss Plant?" I said. "It was me who put the cannon under the Mayor's throne. And that's not all. It was me who locked Dom in the cupboard and made Ruby fall down the trapdoor, too. I did it all myself. I'm sorry I wrecked your play."

Her eyes bugged out of her head with anger. She waved her fists at me.

"You – you won't get away with this!! You're going to be so expelled, it will make your head spin!"

The ambulance doors closed, cutting off her rants, and drove away. Robyn stared at me.

"Hang on – you're taking the blame for all of us?"

I nodded. "I've done a lot of terrible things tonight – it's time I made up for them."

Frank gasped. "Nick, no! They're going to kick you out of school!"

I turned to face Frank – and hugged him.

"Frank, I should have listened to you. You were right all along – you've always been right. And you've always been a good friend to me, too. This is the least I can do to thank you."

I turned to Robyn.

"Robyn, you're an evil genius. If you didn't waste so much time being a pest, you could probably run this school! Why don't you try doing that instead? You can start by taking my place as lunch monitor."

Robyn tapped her chin. "Now that you mention it, telling people what to do *does* sound like fun ..."

I turned to Petra, Taylor, Tomi and Leo.

"Guys, you were great tonight! But I don't think you should ever try doing a prank again. You're hopeless at it."

"Agreed," they said.

"I don't think we'll ever need to prank anyone again," said Petra. "Haven't you seen? Everyone loves us!"

It was true. After their star turns in the play, people were taking notice of them for the first time. And they weren't the only ones who were popular now. Everyone who walked past me was patting me on the back and shaking my hand.

"Great acting, Nick!"

"Nick, you were hilarious!"

"Why don't you explode a confetti cannon at my house this weekend, Nick?"

It was amazing to hear people remember my name. All my life, I had wanted people to take me seriously, but it turned out I was much better at making people laugh. Maybe being a big joke wasn't so bad after all. For the first time in my life, I felt like the star of the show.

But I felt terrible, too. Because there was one person who needed an apology more than anyone else.

I turned around. Jessie stood next to Blake on the playing field behind me. Blake was still staring at his phone, but Jessie's eyes were red from crying. She glared at me as I walked towards her.

"What do *you* want?" she said.

I coughed.

"I came to say sorry for everything I've done." I turned to Blake first. I owed him an apology too. "Blake, I'm sorry for trying to make you look stupid. I was jealous of you for being so popular ... but the truth is you're a much nicer person than I am."

Blake shrugged. "That's OK. Thanks for trying to save my life, at least."

I turned to Jessie.

"And as for you, Jessie – I feel so bad. I'm really sorry. I wasn't trying to ruin your night.

I was just trying to make you like me. But I was so caught up in what *I* wanted, that I didn't think about what *you* wanted at all. Will you ever forgive me?"

She gave me a disgusted look. "No, I won't."

I nodded. I understood completely. "Good luck at your next school. You're a great actor. I hope the people there treat you more nicely than I did."

And with that, I walked back to Frank and the others. Jessie was still angry at me – and who could blame her? – but I felt loads better. Something inside me had changed tonight. I didn't even feel that bad about the thought of being expelled. It was time I had a fresh start – a chance to become a new me, who made people laugh instead of cry.

"Well, we've probably got about half an hour before you're expelled," said Frank. "What shall we do?"

I looked around. Despite everything that had happened that night, people seemed to be having a nice time. The parents were standing around and chatting, and little kids were racing between their legs. The rest of the cast were happily running around in their costumes, their stage fright gone. All the trees around the school had been lit up with twinkling fairy lights, and there was a gentle breeze in the summer evening air. The night was filled with the sound of laughter.

"Let's have some fun," I said. "I think we've had enough romance for one evening, don't you?"

I took my friends' hands, and we ran into the trees, giggling and chasing each other.

It was like some wonderful dream.

Watch out for Ross Montgomery's next hilarious Shakespeare-inspired tale of mishap and mayhem, this time inspired by *The Tempest*:

Our books are tested
for children and young people by
children and young people.

Thanks to everyone who consulted on
a manuscript for their time and effort in
helping us to make our books better
for our readers.